serial romancer

Trevor Millum

Folens

© 2003 Folens Limited, on behalf of the author.
United Kingdom: Folens Publishers, Apex Business Centre, Boscombe
Road, Dunstable, LU5 4RL.
Email: folens@folens.com

Ireland: Folens Publishers, Greenhills Road, Tallaght, Dublin 24.
Email: info@folens.ie

Poland: JUKA, ul. Renesansowa 38, Warsaw 01-905.

Editor: Kay Macmullan
Layout artist: Lee Williams
Cover design: Duncan McTeer
Illustrations: Josephine Blake

First published 2003 by Folens Limited.

British Library Cataloguing in Publication Data. A catalogue record for
this publication is available from the British Library.

ISBN 1 84303 395–X

Contents

The story so far

If you haven't read an *On the edge* **book before:**
The stories take place in and around a row
of shops and buildings called Pier Parade in
Brightsea, right next to the sea. There's Big Fry,
the fish and chip shop; Drop Zone, the drop-in
centre for local teenagers; Macmillan's, the sweet
and souvenir shop; Anglers' Haven, the fishing
tackle shop; the Surf 'n' Skate shop and, of
course, the Brightsea Beach Bar.

If you have read an *On the edge* **book** you may
have met some of these people before.

Phil Johnson: *his mum, Maggie, runs the fish and
chip shop with Phil's step-dad, Ken.*

Vicki Johnson: *Phil's older sister; she goes to college.*

So, what's been going on?
It's usually Phil who ends up in trouble, as he
did when he visited the old pier that night with
Mick. Now, the attention turns to Vicki, who's
had more boyfriends than hot dinners.

What happens in this story?
Phil decides to follow his sister when she goes
out with her new boyfriend. He wants to put
his mum's mind at rest, but what should he do
when he discovers the truth?

4

1

Going out

"That'll be him," said Vicki, picking up her bag. "See you later."

"Remember what I said!" called Mum.

"Yeah. Don't worry, Mum, we're only going round to Gina's."

"Hmm," was all Mum said.
As if going round to Gina's might be as bad as a week at Satan's Black Arts Night Scene.

My sister, Vicki, had a new boyfriend.
I didn't know where she had met him.
I'd only seen him through the window of the chip shop.
He was dark and tall – he could have been Spanish or Italian.

Mum did not approve, but Vicki was
sixteen and a half – and not someone you
could tell what to do.
Mum did tell her, of course, but in a
tactful way.
No point in having a bust-up.

And anyway, we didn't do that in
our family.
Well, not much.

Ken would talk to her as well – but
"It's not easy when it's not your own
daughter," he would say.
And he was right.
Even I had reminded him that he wasn't
our real father once, when he'd tried to
give me a piece of his mind.

"Trouble is, she's half an adult and half a
kid," Mum would say. "Thinks she knows
it all – but she doesn't. Mind you, I was
the same at her age."
She would say all this to no one
in particular.
I knew she worried though.

She couldn't settle until Vicki was back home safely.

Tonight I thought I might help.
I had been in Mum's bad books too often.
I needed a result.
I had seen enough films to know about tailing people.
I could just check up on Vicki, make sure she was going where she said she was going.

I had planned ahead.
I was going round to Jed's to go through some homework.
Mum approved of this.
She didn't think it was 'cheating' or 'copying' like some mums did.
She'd done the same thing when she was at school – working with her friends.
"It made the boring bits better," she said.
And, in any case, she said Jed was better than Mick.
She quite liked Mick, but he was trouble.

So Jed got the thumbs up.
And I had my reason for going out.

As Vicki closed the door, I picked up
my folder.
"OK, I'll be off too. I won't be late."
"You are going to Jed's, aren't you, Phil?"
said Mum.
"Yes, Mum …"
She started to say something else, but I
interrupted.
"No, Mum, Mick won't be there."
She relaxed – almost.
I took my chance to leave.

Ken was already in the shop, preparing
the fish.
I slipped out of the side door.

2

On the trail

Once I was outside, I could see Vicki and
the boyfriend at the end of the parade.
I waited to see which way they turned
and then I walked quickly to the corner.
There were quite a few other people
about, which made it easy.
I don't know how you tail someone when
you're the only other person around.
Especially if you happen to be
her brother!

They climbed the steps to the main road,
crossed and set off down Ware Street, as I
had expected.
Then down Trinity Road but, instead of
turning left, they went right.
I was on to something.
Gina did not live in that direction.

There were even more people about now.
It made it easier to hide – but more
difficult to keep them in sight.
I was glad when they stopped.
They were looking in the window of a CD
and video shop.
It gave me a chance to pause and think.

Vicki thought I was too young to be of any interest.
And Mum still didn't really trust me.
Well, I would show them both.
I could be the one to stop Vicki being taken away by a gang of Hell's Angels.
I could prevent her running off with drug smugglers.
I could raise the alarm when …
Well, when anything bad happened.

I was ready.

I was so busy with my thoughts that I almost lost Vicki and her boyfriend.
Just in time, I saw them turning back down Church Street.
I was quick.
I was on their trail.

I was disappointed when they carried on down The Avenue.
It meant that they were going to Gina's after all.
What a let down!

3

Telling Jed

I didn't fancy hanging around in the street
outside Gina's house.
If I'd had a car, it might have been different.
I sighed and headed on down to Jed's.
I'd told him I might call in – but I had been
careful not to say exactly when.

Jed opened the door.
He was wearing rubber gloves.
"Hi, Phil," he said. "What've you
been doing?"

"Let me come in and I'll tell you," I said.
Jed and I went through to the kitchen.
There was a pile of washing-up.
Jed took off his washing-up gloves.
Jed didn't care whether he looked cool or not.
"Got to protect my hands," he said.

"Anyway, what've you been up to?"

"Tailing Sis," I said.

"What?"

"Following her," I explained. "Mum gets worried when she goes out with a new boyfriend. I thought I'd follow them. Just check up that they were going where she said – to Gina's."
Now I explained it, it sounded weak and a bit silly.

"What if she didn't?" asked Jed. "You gonna tell your mum? That's a bit mean, innit?"

"I dunno. I suppose so. Depends where they go."

Jed said nothing.
I could tell he thought I was stupid.
Maybe he was right.

"Maybe I'd just let her know what I'd found out," I wondered aloud.

"Yeah. You could blackmail her then. Bet she's got lots of dosh from working in that shop in town."

Was Jed being funny?
I didn't fancy myself as a blackmailer.
They usually end up in a ditch with a knife in their back.
Not that I thought Vicki would kill me.
Not exactly.
But something close to it.

"Never mind," I said. "I could keep it to myself. Knowledge is power."

Jed put his washing-up gloves on again.
He started to scrub the frying pan.

I didn't realise I was that boring.

4

Sister tracking

I didn't give up – even though Jed had made me think a bit.

I followed Vicki and Robert a few times.
He was a student at the language college.
They didn't go anywhere interesting.
They didn't do anything odd.
Usually they visited Vicki's friends.
Once they went to the 3 Bs bar.

"I'm helping him with his English," Vicki said to Mum.

"I bet you are," she said.
But she smiled to show she wasn't being nasty.
"And is his English getting better?"

"Course it is. You can't stop him talking sometimes."

This seemed to please Mum for some reason.
"Are we going to meet him?"

Vicki looked doubtful.
"I dunno. He's shy."

"Just bring him in the shop for a bag of chips," said Ken. "That's a good way of saying hello."

"I might do that," said Vicki. "Yeah."

5

New boy

Vicki did come into the shop – but not
with Robert.
She drifted in one evening with a
fair-haired bloke.
He had a bit of a beard and a stud
through his eyebrow.
Mum was serving.
She stopped and stared.

"Hi, Mum," said Vicki. "This is Steve.
Can we have some chips?"

Mum recovered quickly.
"Hi, Steve. Do you want anything
with them?"

Steve opened his mouth but Vicki spoke.
"No – just salt and vinegar. Cheers, Mum.
See you later!"
Then she was gone.

Steve had said nothing – just given a kind
of nod and half a smile.

I could tell Mum wanted to ask questions.
But how could she?

I followed them.

They walked all the way along the front,
eating chips as they went.
Then they stood looking at the sea.
They looked as if they had known each
other for ages.
 "Right," I thought. "Another new bloke.
I'll keep my eye on this one."

6

Developments

Nothing happened for a couple of weeks.
I didn't follow them every time they
went out.
I didn't have enough excuses to do that.
But one Friday evening they met up near
the pier.

I was there.
Twenty metres away.
I hid behind one of the groynes on
the beach.

I saw him give her a floppy disk.
She put it away quickly.
Then they walked on down the seafront.

What was going on?

I made sure I was there when she came in.

"Hello, love," said Mum. "Have a good evening?"

"Great, thanks," said Vicki.
She smiled and chatted for a while.

Then she went off to her room.
I heard her switch her computer on.
It was a second-hand one Ken had got for her from a mate at the cash and carry.
It wasn't super-fast, but it worked most of the time.
It was even connected to the Internet, although Vicki had to use it after 6 pm when it was cheap.

Maybe it was a disk of hers she'd left with Steve, and he was giving it back?

I was curious – but then I forgot about it.
There were plenty of possible explanations.

7

More questions than answers

But then it happened again.

About ten days later – another disk.

I'd never have seen it, but I got lucky.

Vicki dropped it from her bag as she
came in.

The way she picked it up told me it was
like the last one.

Suspicious.

Once again, nothing was said.

Now I was really curious.

Vicki was acting oddly too – spending
much more time in her room.

Getting on with her college work,
she said.

That evening I went round to Jed's again.
But I couldn't concentrate on what Jed
was saying.

He looked at me once or twice as if to say,
"What's up with you?"
But he didn't say it.
He only had to wait.

In the end I said, "There's something
odd going on. With Vicki – and
her latest bloke."
"What do you mean 'odd'?"

"Why does she never bring him home?
Why do they have these meetings out on
the front? And what's on those disks?"
"What disks?"

"She meets him and then he slips her
these disks. She doesn't say anything
about it."
"Could be anything. You just think you're
some kind of spy. You make stuff up."

I didn't argue.
He could be right.
But … there *was* something odd.

8

Found out

The next time I followed them I made a
big mistake.
I got too close.
And I stayed out too long.
I wanted to get a closer look.
I wanted to make sure of what I saw.

They walked a long way that night.
All the way down to the marina.

When I got home I was amazed.
Vicki was already there.
She must have taken a taxi or something.

"Where have you been?" asked Mum.

"Just ... round at Jed's ..." I said.

"I called," said Mum. "You weren't there."

I didn't like the look on her face.
I had become lazy.
I hadn't covered my tracks.
Now I was trying to find an excuse.
My mind tried to get a grip but it couldn't
find anything.

Then something even worse happened.

"I know where he's been!" snapped
my sister.

We both turned and stared at her.

"What?" cried Mum.

"I know where he's been. He's been
spying on me, the little sneak. Following
me and Steve. Trying to catch us snogging
were you? Would that be nice? You little
pervert!"

I just stood there.
I was stunned.
How could she?
Did she really think that?
Or was she using this to cover up
her secret?
What if I told them what I'd seen?

They were both looking at me.

But I had no proof.
And it was half true, anyway.
I had been following them.

"I was just keeping an eye on them," I
said. "I knew you were worried … So,
I just …"

"Spied on us!" Vicki finished the sentence
for me.

Mum looked at me.
She seemed puzzled.
"None of this makes sense to me,"
she said.

She looked at Vicki and then back at me.
"You get to bed," she said. "I don't want
you late for school again. We'll talk about
this tomorrow."

I was glad to leave.
No doubt she and Vicki would
discuss me.
Vicki would use the time to make sure
Mum believed her.
It would not be difficult.
After all, I *had* been following her.
It had seemed like a good idea.
It had seemed fun.
But it wasn't as easy as I had thought.

9

Thinking it through

That night I thought about Vicki and
the disks.
There *was* something going on.
Maybe it was harmless.
Maybe not.

The first thing anyone thinks is –
the Internet.
Downloading stuff.
Stuff you don't want your parents – or
little brother – to see.

I could ask her.
I could search her room.
I didn't like either idea – but I fell asleep
thinking about it.

The following morning Mum cornered me.

"I don't want you following Vicki,"
she said.
I shrugged.
"All right," I said.

"You may have meant well," she went
on. "Or not. I don't know what goes on in
your head sometimes. But a girl does *not*
want to be trailed round town by
her brother."

"OK," I said. "I've got the message."

I didn't mind that much.
It was getting boring anyway.
It was only the disks that interested me.
And Vicki's new study habits.

I thought again about searching
Vicki's room.
Checking her computer.
It would be easy.
I was always home before her.
Mum and Ken were usually too busy in
the shop to see what I was doing.
I could easily search the cupboards and
drawers too.

But I wasn't going to take any risks.

Vicki's insults were bad enough.
If she caught me – or if Mum caught me
going through her things – BANG!
That would be it.
Just think what she would say if she
found me looking in the drawer where
she kept her underwear.
'Pervert' would be too mild.

And what if she spread it around school?
She still had friends there.
I felt hot.

No, Jed would help me.

10

Detective work

Jed stood at the top of the stairs.
"All right," he said. "But I think you're mad. Just don't take too long."

That was the problem.
Search Vicki's room?
It just wasn't that easy.
In the films, they never have to wade through piles of papers on the floor.
Or heaps of magazines and CDs out of their cases.
There were even soft toys piled in a corner – including a green hippo.
It was awful.
I tried the usual places – including the underwear drawer.
Nothing.

Then I remembered Vicki's college stuff.
Hmm.
I didn't want to look there – too many
papers and folders.
I lifted the first folder.
A black disk fell out.
Bingo!

The door opened.
I dropped the disk and whirled round.

It was Jed.

I breathed a sigh of relief.

"How much longer are you going to be?"

"Not long! Now get back out there. What if someone comes?"

I slipped the disk into the computer and waited while the folders came up
on screen.
They were *Word* files.
I opened one.
At first I didn't know what to make of it.
'Assignment 4.'
And a name – Stefan somebody – a name I couldn't pronounce.
And then I saw what Vicki was doing.
Of course!

I slipped the disk back into the folder.
I put it back exactly where it was.
I looked round.
All was as it should be – a mess.

I left the room just as I heard Jed say, "Oh, I was just going, Mrs Johnson!"
Not the right words!
Not the code we had agreed!
But it gave me enough time to close the door and join him on the landing.

Downstairs, Mum offered Jed a drink.
"Go on!" I said. "You can stay a bit longer."
I wanted to talk to him.

"Case solved?" asked Jed, once Mum had gone.
"Mmm," I said.
"Is that a yes?"
"Sort of."
"Anything exciting?"
"No. Not exactly. It's funny, really."
"Funny?"
"Well, Vicki wasn't that good at school. At least, she made out that she wasn't. She's not daft, though. And now she's the expert."
"Eh?"

"She said she was helping Robert with his English."

"Robert?"

"The last boyfriend. She gets through them fast. Now she's doing more than that. For Steven – or Stefan …"

"What do you mean?"

"She's doing the work for him. Stuff he should be doing. Yes! Now I see!"

"What?"

"That's why she doesn't bring him in. That's why he never said anything. His English is too poor. He's probably having a really hard time."

"And Vicki's helping him?"

"Yeah. She fancies him. Maybe they're already going out. So he's got her to do the hard work instead. Well, maybe not all of it. She's such a mug."

"Hmm."

I could see Jed was losing interest.

"Thanks for helping," I said.

"No problem."

11

Caught out

Let it go, I thought.
What does it matter?
He'll get found out in time.
He might get a diploma from the college.
He might go back home with a bit
of paper.
So what?

I walked back to Jed's place with him.
Then I wandered home along the front.
The lights were on.
The season was drawing to a close but
there were still plenty of visitors.
I liked the pier lights best.
I never got tired of them.

As I stood and watched, I saw someone
I knew.
Who was it?

I got closer and then I recognised him.
Fair hair.
The stud in the eyebrow.
Steve!
Or Stefan.
Whatever his name was.
And not on his own.

He had his arm round someone else.
It could be his sister – but no.
That hug was not a brotherly hug.

And where was Vicki?
Probably at home doing *his* homework …

I had another careful look.
There was no doubt.
I set off home, wondering.
What was I going to do now?

I imagined what Vicki would say if I told
her what I'd seen.

"So you're spying on him now, are
you?" or "Why should I believe you?"
or "What's up with you? Just can't stand
him, can you? You'll make anything up
to get at me."

No one likes to be told bad news.
No one likes to be made a fool of.
And no one likes the person who brings
bad news.

12

Talking to little brother

I nearly chickened out.
I didn't say anything that evening.

The following night, at about nine o'clock,
Vicki came in.
I heard her come up to her room.
I wasn't spying, but I saw her carrying
another disk.
More homework from two-timing Steve!

I felt really angry with him.
I also felt cross with her.
All the names she'd called me – why should
I feel sorry for her?
But I did.
She was family.
And most of the time we got on pretty well.

Still, I might not have said anything.
But she knocked on my door – knocked!
She didn't always do that!

She looked a bit shame-faced.
Then she said, "Phil, you're good at
English. Which of these do you think
is right:

*'The rest of the group went on ahead so the
goodbyes were left to John and me. Or, John
and I'?*

I looked at her.
"Hmm," I said, pretending to think.
Then I said, "Is it a question from a
magazine quiz?"

She looked startled.
"Er – yes. 'How Good is Your English?'"

"Well, you'll never know if you ask me."

"Oh, don't be mean."
She glared at me, and turned to go.

"Why don't you just do the quiz and then look up the answers? Tell you what, I'll have a go after you and we can compare."

She paused for a moment.
I think she nearly flounced off.
But something made her stay.

"What is it really?" I asked.

Again she paused.
"It's something I'm doing for a friend."
"Steve?"
"Yes, if you must know."

"I'll give you a hand," I said, "but when you give him the disk back with his corrected work on, ask him who he was with last night."

Her eyes grew wide.
For a moment I thought she was going to hit me.
Then she turned and went out.
A moment later I heard her using her mobile.
Soon after that she ran downstairs.

13

Final act

I couldn't resist.
This time I had to follow.
I didn't bother with an excuse.
Ken and Mum were busy in the shop.
I just slipped out of the side door.
Vicki was at the corner by the time I hit
the pavement.

There was a disk in her right hand.
She was twirling it in her fingers, as if it
were red-hot.

I almost pitied Steve.
I hoped he had some good excuses.

Then she disappeared, racing down the
parade and I lost sight of her.
But I thought I knew where she would
meet him.

It was almost dark and I managed to keep
in the shadows.
I dodged from shop to shop …
Where *was* she?

It was no good.
I'd lost her.
They weren't where I'd expected.
Now I had no idea where to go.

I decided to walk along the beach and
then go home.
I'd been out long enough.
I crunched across the shingle.
My hood was up in case anyone saw me.

Then I saw them.

Steve was half-sitting, half-lying on the
beach – as if he'd been knocked over.
The girl he'd been with was
standing nearby.
She was keeping well out of things.
Vicki was standing over Steve.

"Here! You can have your stupid disk back!" she was saying. "And the rest!"

She dug into her pocket and pulled out five or six disks.
She flung them at Steve.
He put up his hands to protect his face, but several hit the mark.

"Ow!" he cried.
"And by the way," she added. "Don't bother looking for those last two pieces I checked for you. I deleted them. Like I'm deleting you!"
With that she stomped away from them.

I made myself scarce.

I got home just before she did.
Whatever Steve's English was like, he'd got the message.

14

Back to life

She didn't say anything about Steve – or
about the English she'd done for him.
I thought she would be upset.
So I was especially nice to her the next day.

She didn't seem to notice.

I went off to school and she went off
to college.

The next evening she was in the shop again.
She was with a bloke who had
a moustache.
He looked a good bit older than her.

"This is Mark," she said.
He smiled.
"Good evening," he said.
Mum smiled back.

"What would you like?" she asked.
"Fish and chips to take off, please," he said.
"To take away," corrected Vicki.
He smiled again.
"To take away," he repeated.

"Helping Mark with his English?" asked Mum.

Vicki just smiled.
They walked out together.

I didn't follow.